W9-BGO-763

ELEPHANT LEARNS TO SHARE
A book about SHARING

Written by Sue Graves

Illustrated by Trevor Dunton

Franklin Watts®
An imprint of Scholastic Inc.

Elephant was very selfish. He would not share **anything**. He would not share his candy.

He would not share his toys.

He would not even share his games. He always kept **everything** for himself.

At school, Elephant would not share his
paints, even when Monkey ran out and could
not finish his picture. Elephant said the paints
were **his** and he **did not want** to share.
Monkey thought Elephant was not being nice.

At snack time, Elephant would not share
his snack, even when Hippo forgot to bring
his own snack to school. Elephant said he
wanted his snack **for himself**. Hippo
thought Elephant was not being nice at all.

On Friday, Elephant was really selfish. He would not share any of the books in the library corner. Little Lion said Elephant **did not need** all the books at once. He said Elephant could read only one book at a time. But Elephant said he wanted all the books for himself.

Little Lion told Miss Bird. Miss Bird said Elephant could not stay in the library corner if he did not share nicely.

At recess, Elephant found an old ball under a bush. Everyone wanted to play with it, but Elephant said **he found it**, so it was **his ball** and he did not have to share it if he did not want to. Elephant's friends got **upset**. They thought he was not being nice.

On Saturday morning, Elephant's grandma came to visit. She had a **nice surprise** for Elephant. It was a new baseball set. It had a shiny red ball and a big wooden bat with a bright blue handle. Elephant thought it was the best baseball set in the world.

First, Elephant threw the ball. He threw it really hard. It went really far.

Then Elephant swung the bat. It swung really well. Elephant was very happy.

Next, Elephant tried to throw
the ball . . . **and hit it**.
But he could not do it.

Then he tried to hit the ball . . .
and catch it. But he could
not do that either.

Elephant was **not happy**.
His new baseball set was
no fun at all.

Elephant went to find his friends. They were by the swamp. They were playing with an old baseball set. The ball was not shiny at all and the bat's handle was bent and broken—but **everyone** was having lots of fun.

Elephant told his friends about his new baseball set. He told them about the shiny red ball and the big wooden bat with the bright blue handle, but no one was interested. They were having too much fun **playing together** with the old set.

Then Elephant asked if he could play, too. But everyone said **no**. They said he did not share with them **ever**! So they did not want to share their game with him. Elephant went home. He felt very sad.

Elephant saw Grandma in the yard. She asked why he was sad. Elephant told her that his friends did not want to share with him because he never shared with them. He said he wished he could **make things right**. Grandma told him to think about how to do that.

Elephant thought about it. He said he should say **sorry** to his friends for being so **selfish**. He said he should **ask** his friends to come and play with his new baseball set. Grandma said that those were good ideas.

Elephant found his friends. He said he was **sorry** for not sharing with them. He promised never to be selfish again. Then he asked them if they would like to come and play baseball at his house. Everyone said **yes**.

Everyone liked Elephant's new baseball set.
They liked the shiny red ball and the big
wooden bat with the bright blue handle.

Elephant let everyone
take turns
swinging the bat.

He let everyone
take turns
throwing the ball.

Then they all played a game **together**.
Everyone said it was the best game ever.
Elephant was happy.

Soon it was time for a snack. Grandma had made a large cake with lots of cherries on top. It looked delicious. Elephant cut the cake into slices. He made sure everyone had their **fair share**. He made sure everyone had a cherry, too. He said it was **nicer to share things** with your friends . . . and much **more fun**! Everyone agreed!

A note about sharing this book

The **Behavior Matters** series has been developed to provide a starting point for further discussion on children's behavior both in relation to themselves and others. The series features animal characters reflecting typical behavior traits often seen in young children.

Elephant Learns to Share
This story explores the problems that can occur when children do not share with others and the isolation and loneliness that can follow.

The book aims to encourage children to develop ways of engaging with their peers. It highlights the point that to share is preferable to being lonely and suggests ways in which a child might engage with others.

How to use the book
The book is designed for adults to share with an individual child or a group of children, and as a starting point for discussion.

The book also provides visual support and repeated words and phrases to build reading confidence.

Before reading the story
Choose a time to read when you and the children are relaxed and have time to share the story.

Spend time looking at the illustrations and talk about what the book might be about before reading it together.

Encourage children to tackle new words by sounding them out.

After reading, talk about the book with the children:

- What was the story about? Have the children ever wanted to keep all their toys for themselves? Have they ever resented having to share with brothers, sisters, or friends in class? Encourage them to explain why they were reluctant to share with others. Ask them if playing alone was as much fun as playing with a friend or sibling.

- Extend this by asking the children if anyone has ever refused to share with them. How did they feel? Did they feel angry or upset? Did they think the other person was selfish?

- Talk about the benefits of sharing with others. For example, some games would be impossible to play unless others played, too. Invite the children to think of games and activities that they have especially enjoyed with their friends.

- Take the opportunity to talk about dealing with someone who doesn't want to share. How could the children help someone who doesn't share? Point out that the best way to encourage others to share is to lead by example.

- Talk about the importance of saying sorry to those who have been upset. Explain how this can make the person feel better if someone has refused to share with them.

- Invite children to role-play the parts of Elephant and his friends in the story using the strategies for encouraging Elephant to share that were discussed earlier.

- Encourage the children to work in groups and cooperate on an activity, such as making a building with blocks. Encourage the children to share resources and to ensure that each member of the group is allowed to contribute fully.

Library of Congress Cataloging-in-Publication Data
Names: Graves, Sue, 1950– author. | Dunton, Trevor, illustrator.
Title: Elephant learns to share: a book about sharing/written by Sue Graves; illustrated by Trevor Dunton.
Description: First edition. | New York: Franklin Watts, an imprint of Scholastic Inc., 2021. |
    Series: Behavior matters | Audience: Ages 4–7. | Audience: Grades K–1. | Summary: Elephant does
    not like to share his toys, games, or snacks—but when he gets a new bat and ball he realizes that it is
    no fun trying to play with them by himself, so he asks his grandmother how he can make amends with
    his friends.
Identifiers: LCCN 2021000572 (print) | LCCN 2021000573 (ebook) | ISBN 9781338758078
    (library binding) | ISBN 9781338758085 (paperback) | ISBN 9781338758092 (ebook)
Subjects: LCSH: Elephants—Juvenile fiction. | Animals—Juvenile fiction. | Sharing—Juvenile fiction. |
    Apologizing—Juvenile fiction. | CYAC: Sharing—Fiction. | Elephants—Fiction. | Animals—Fiction.
Classification: LCC PZ7.G7754 El 2021 (print) | LCC PZ7.G7754 (ebook) | DDC [E]—dc23
LC record available at https://lccn.loc.gov/2021000572
LC ebook record available at https://lccn.loc.gov/2021000573

First published in Great Britain in 2015
by The Watts Publishing Group
Published in the United States in 2022
by Scholastic Inc.

10 9 8 7 6 5 4 3 2 1   22 23 24 25 26 27

Printed in China
First edition, 2022